Go to Sleep, Dear Dragon

by Margaret Hillert

Illustrated by Jack Pullan

NORWOOD HOUSE PRESS

DEAR CAREGIVER,

The books in this Beginning-to-Read collection may look somewhat familiar in that the original versions could have been a part of your own early reading experiences. These carefully written texts feature common sight words to provide your child multiple exposures to the words appearing most frequently in written text. These new versions have been updated and the engaging illustrations are highly appealing to a contemporary audience of young readers.

Begin by reading the story to your child, followed by letting him or her read familiar words and soon your child will be able to read the story independently. At each step of the way, be sure to praise your reader's efforts to build his or her confidence as an independent reader. Discuss the pictures and encourage your child to make connections between the story and his or her own life. At the end of the story, you will find reading activities and a word list that will help your child practice and strengthen beginning reading skills. These activities, along with the comprehension questions are aligned to current standards, so reading efforts at home will directly support the instructional goals in the classroom.

Above all, the most important part of the reading experience is to have fun and enjoy it!

Shannon Cannon,
Literacy Consultant

Norwood House Press • www.norwoodhousepress.com
Beginning-to-Read™ is a registered trademark of Norwood House Press.
Illustration and cover design copyright ©2017 by Norwood House Press. All Rights Reserved.

Authorized adapted reprint from the U.S. English language edition, entitled Go to Sleep, Dear Dragon by Margaret Hillert. Copyright © 2017 Margaret Hillert. Reprinted with permission. All rights reserved. Pearson and Go to Sleep, Dear Dragon are trademarks, in the US and/or other countries, of Pearson Education, Inc. or its affiliates. This publication is protected by copyright, and prior permission to re-use in any way in any format is required by both Norwood House Press and Pearson Education. This book is authorized in the United States for use in schools and public libraries.

Paperback ISBN: 978-1-60357-879-0
The Library of Congress has cataloged the hardcover edition of this book with the following call number: 2015046746

290N—072016
Printed in Shenzhen, Guangdong, China.

Go to sleep, Dear Dragon.
Go to sleep.
This is a good thing
for us to do.

Look here.
Look here.
This one is big!
It is not my house.

I will go in.
I will go in to see
what I can see.

Oh, my.
Oh, my.
What have we here?
It looks like fun.

I see this.
I see that.
I can look—
 and look—
  and look.

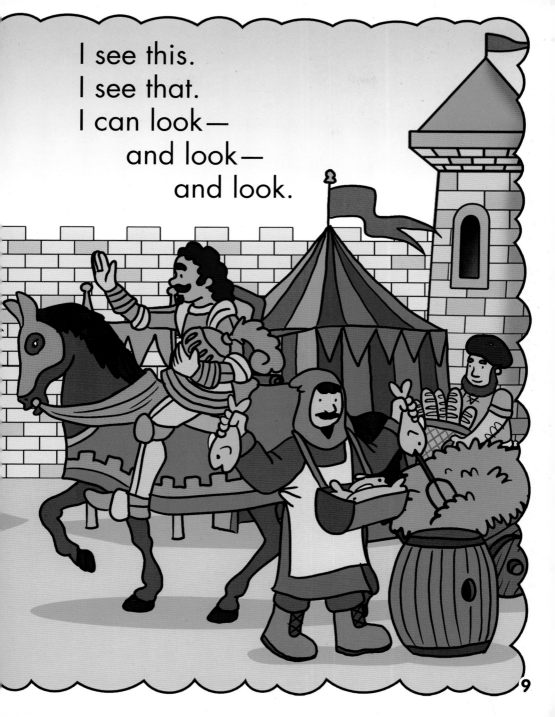

9

Look at this man.
See what he can do.
He is good.

And look here.
One, two, three.
One is down.
Two are up, up, up.

And what is this?
What do I see now?

One man is up.
One man is down.

He is good.
He will get something.
Something pretty.

Here is a pretty little one.
It can run and jump.
I like this one.
What fun this is!

But I have to go now.
Mother and Father will want me.
I will go to my house.

That is funny.
I see something.
But what is it?
I can not make it out.

And what do I see here?
Here is something big.
Big, big, big.

I guess no one wants it.
No one is here.
No one can see it but me.

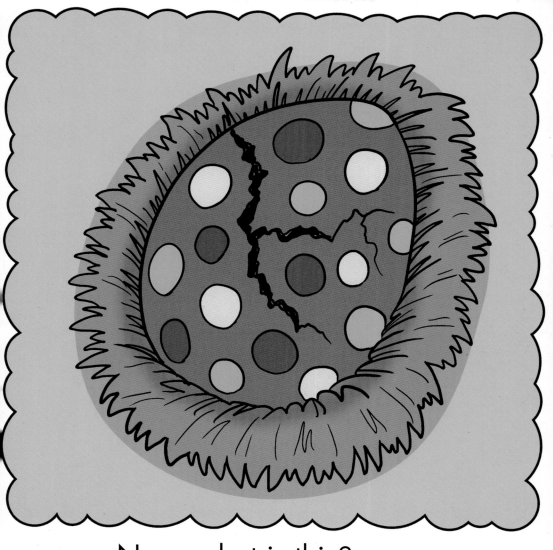

Now, what is this?
Look here. Look here.
Look at this.
Something will come out.

21

Oh, my!
Oh my!
A baby dragon!
A little baby dragon.

Oh, how little you are!
But you will get big.

24

You can play with me.
We can have fun.

I like you.
I want you with me.
Come to my house.
I will find something
good for you to eat.

Here you are with me.
And here I am with you.
Oh, what a happy dream,
Dear Dragon.

READING REINFORCEMENT

The following activities support the findings of the National Reading Panel that determined the most effective components for reading instruction are: Phonemic Awareness, Phonics, Vocabulary, Fluency, and Text Comprehension.

Phonemic Awareness: The /sl/ sound

Oddity Task: Say the /**sl**/ sound for your child. Ask your child to say the word that doesn't begin with the /**sl**/ sound in the following word groups:

ship, slip, sleep	sled, sad, slide	slick, sling, spot
sat, slim, sled,	slice, sign, sleeve	slate, see, sliver
slow, slug, shake	something, slant, slipper	

Phonics: The letter Kk

1. Demonstrate how to form the letters **K** and **k** for your child.
2. Have your child practice writing **K** and **k** at least three times each.
3. Ask your child to point to the words in the book that have the letter **k** in them.
4. Explain to your child that when the letter **k** is followed by the letter **n** it is silent—doesn't make a sound.
5. Write the words listed below and ask your child to point to them and repeat them.

know	knight	knock	knit	knee
knob	knife	knuckle	knot	knead

6. Say the words in random order and ask your child to point to the right word.
7. Ask your child to read the words he or she can from the list.

Vocabulary: Story Words

1. Write the following words on separate pieces of paper and point to them as you read them to your child:

   castle   dragon   jester   knight   princess

2. Say the following sentences aloud and ask your child to point to the word that is described:

   - Once upon a time there was a big, beautiful place where the king and queen lived. (castle)
   - The man on the horse who had shiny armor was called a (knight).
   - The daughter of the king and queen was called a (princess).
   - What hatched out of the egg that the boy found in his dream? (dragon)
   - The funny man who juggled the balls in the air is called a what? (jester)

Fluency: Echo Reading

1. Reread the story to your child at least two more times while your child tracks the print by running a finger under the words as they are read. Ask your child to read the words he or she knows with you.

2. Reread the story, stopping after each sentence or page to allow your child to read (echo) what you have read. Repeat echo reading and let your child take the lead.

Text Comprehension: Discussion Time

1. Ask your child to retell the sequence of events in the story.

2. To check comprehension, ask your child the following questions:

   - Why do you think the words and pictures in this story are in bubbles? (to help the reader understand that the boy is dreaming)
   - If you lived during the time of the dream, which character would you like to be? Why?

WORD LIST

Go to Sleep, Dear Dragon uses the 73 words listed below.

This list can be used to practice reading the words that appear in the text. You may wish to write the words on index cards and use them to help your child build automatic word recognition. Regular practice with these words will enhance your child's fluency in reading connected text.

a	eat	I	oh	up
am		in	one	us
and	Father	is	out	
are	find	it		want(s)
at	for		play	we
	fun	jump	pretty	what
baby	funny			where
big		like	run	will
but	get	little		with
	go	look(s)	see	
can	good		sleep	you
come	guess	make	something	
		man	spot	
dear	happy	me		
did	have	Mother	that	
do	he	my	thing	
down	here		this	
dragon	house	no	three	
dream	how	not	to	
		now	two	

ABOUT THE AUTHOR Margaret Hillert has helped millions of children all over the world learn to read independently. She was a first grade teacher for 34 years and during that time started writing books that her students could both gain confidence in reading and enjoy. She wrote well over 100 books for children just learning to read. As a child, she enjoyed writing poetry and continued her poetic writings as an adult for both children and adults.

Photograph by Glenna Washburn

ABOUT THE ILLUSTRATOR A talented and creative illustrator, Jack Pullan, is a graduate of William Jewell College. He has also studied informally at Oxford University and the Kansas City Art Institute. He was mentored by the renowned watercolor artists, Jim Hamil and Bill Amend. Jack's work has graced the pages of many enjoyable children's books, various educational materials, cartoon strips, as well as many greeting cards. Jack currently resides in Kansas.